#22
Palms-Rancho Park Branch Library
2920 Overland Avenue
Los Angeles, CA 90064

# THE BOY & THE BINDI

ARSENAL
PULP PRESS

# THE BOY & THE BINDI

WRITTEN BY
**Vivek Shraya**

ILLUSTRATED BY
**RAJNI PERERA**

Have you seen my Ammi's dot?
It's a bright and pretty spot.

Her dot comes in every hue.
She likes red and sometimes blue.

She peels and pastes it like a sticker
Gently with her thumb and finger.

Above her nose is where it goes.
What is this dot? I want to know!

*Ammi, why do you wear that dot?*
*What's so special about that spot?*

**It's not a dot,** says my **Ammi**—
*It's not a spot, it's a bindi!*

What's a bindi? What does it do?

My bindi keeps me safe and true.

*How does it do that, Ammi, how?*

*Well, when I stick it on my brow*

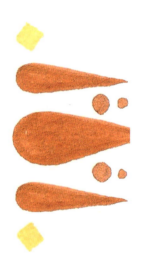

My bindi tells me where I'm from.
My bindi reminds me of my mom
And when she gave me my first one.

I look at her bindi with this view—
I too would like to be safe and true.
*Ammi, can I have a bindi to wear?*
*Do you have one more to spare?*

She smiles and reaches in her drawer.
*Ta-da!* she says. *This one is yours!*

She sticks it on my bare forehead

But in the mirror, I don't see red.
What a surprise to discover
Yellow is my bindi's colour!

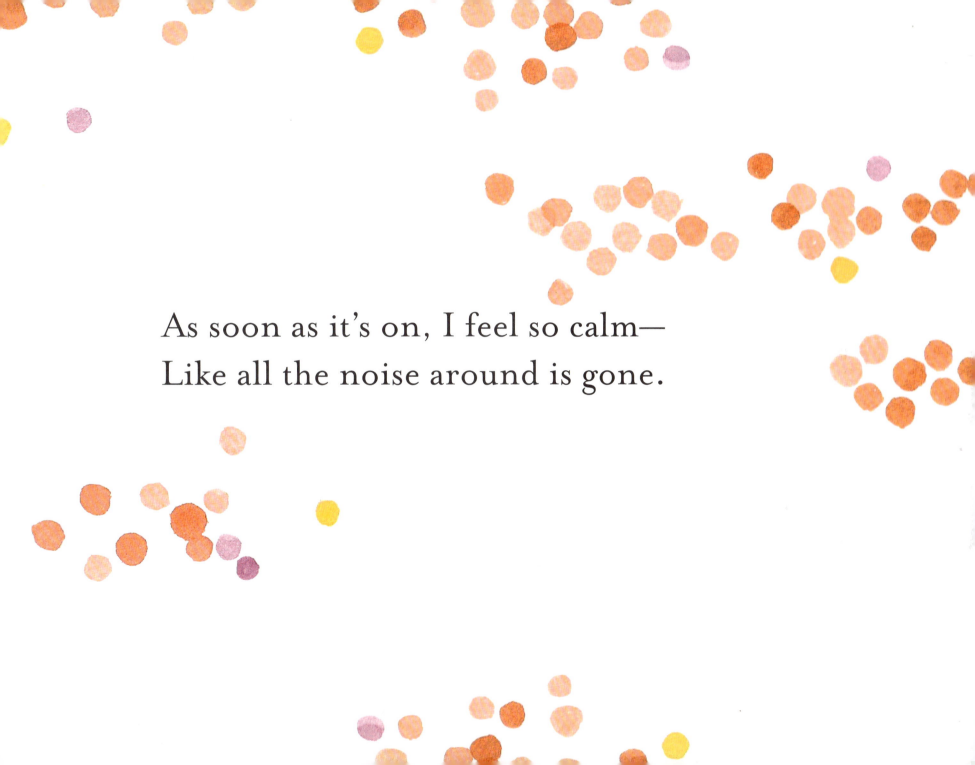

As soon as it's on, I feel so calm—
Like all the noise around is gone.

But when I'm outside, people stare.

Maybe they want a bindi to wear?

My friends at school all want to know:

*What is that dot above your nose?*

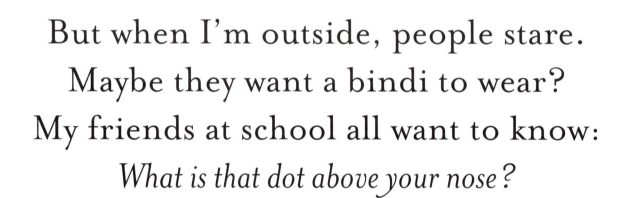

I do not have the words to say
But if I close my eyes and wait
My bindi turns into a star, and then
My forehead turns into the sky, that's when
All my fears fade out of sight
And my body feels so light—
Ammi was so very right!

So now I leave it on my face.
My bindi will always have its place.
When I bathe or go to bed
My bindi stays on my forehead.

Not just because of the glue
Or because it keeps me true—
But sometimes I've felt small like a dot
And sometimes ugly like a blot.

But if a bindi can be more than a spot

And bring beauty where there was not

Maybe I can too…

Have you seen my yellow dot?

It's a bindi, not a spot.

*Why do you wear a bindi?* you say.

*Why is it so special anyway?*

Well, my bindi is like a third eye

Watching over me all the time

Making sure I don't hide

Everything I am inside

And everything that I can be.

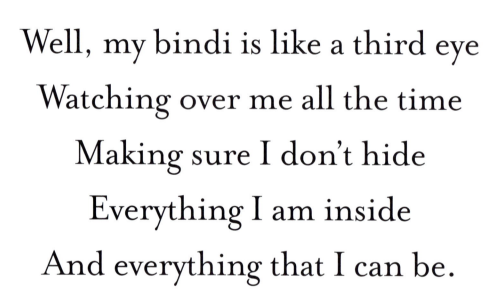

Thank you Ammi, for my bindi!

**VIVEK SHRAYA** is a Toronto-based artist whose body of work includes several albums, films, and books including *God Loves Hair*, *She of the Mountains*, and *even this page is white*. Vivek is a three-time Lambda Literary Award finalist, a 2015 Toronto Arts Foundation Emerging Artist Award finalist, and a 2015 recipient of the Writers' Trust of Canada's Dayne Ogilvie Prize Honour of Distinction.

## VIVEK'S THANKS

This book would not be possible without Brian Lam and Arsenal Pulp Press (Robert Ballantyne, Susan Safyan, Cynara Geissler & Oliver McPartlin) who took a chance on a children's picture book, and genius Rajni Perera, who brought these words to life.

This book would also not be possible without guidance and enthusiasm from Shemeena Shraya, Adam Holman, Trisha Yeo, Cory Silverberg, Robin Phillips, Meghan Park, Guy Weadick School, Kristin Russo, Rachna Contractor, Farzana Doctor, Amber Dawn, Tonya Martin, Evan Munday, Katherine Friesen, Karen Campos Castillo, Alanna Chelmick, Talya Macedo, Shamik, and Dad.

Special thank you to my dear Ammi for being the eternal source of my gender inspiration.

**RAJNI PERERA** is an artist living and working in Toronto, Canada. She uses an immigrant perspective to make work about the coloured female body and its place in visual, science fiction/fantasy, and popular culture.

## RAJNI'S THANKS

To my daughter Sayuri, destined to save the world. And to my mother Sharmini, who changed things with her love.

*For an audio recording of* The Boy & the Bindi
*along with a free teacher's guide
(developed by educators Robin Phillips and Meghan Park):*
vivekshraya.com/bindi
*or* arsenalpulp.com

THE BOY & THE BINDI
Copyright © 2016 by Vivek Shraya

ARSENAL PULP PRESS
Suite 202 – 211 East Georgia St.
Vancouver, BC V6A 1Z6
Canada
*arsenalpulp.com*

The publisher gratefully acknowledges the support of the Canada Council for the Arts and the British Columbia Arts Council for its publishing program, and the Government of Canada (through the Canada Book Fund) and the Government of British Columbia (through the Book Publishing Tax Credit Program) for its publishing activities.

Illustrations by Rajni Perera
Design by Oliver McPartlin

Printed and bound in Canada

Library and Archives Canada Cataloguing in Publication:

Shraya, Vivek, 1981-, author
     The boy & the bindi / written by Vivek Shraya ; illustrated by Rajni Perera.

Issued in print and electronic formats.
ISBN 978-1-55152-668-3 (hardback).—ISBN 978-1-55152-669-0 (html).—
ISBN 978-1-55152-670-6 (pdf)

     I. Perera, Rajni, 1985-, illustrator  II. Title.  III. Title: Boy and the bindi.

PS8637.H73B69 2016          jC813'.6          C2016-905390-3
                                               C2016-905391-1